SOLOMON'S ROBOT

WRITTEN BY
ADAM GRIFFITH

ILLUSTRATED BY
MAKAYLA PALUMBO

Halo
PUBLISHING
INTERNATIONAL

ISBN: 978-1-61244-828-2
Library of Congress Control Number: 2020903996

Printed in the United States of America

Halo Publishing International
8000 W Interstate 10
Suite 600
San Antonio, Texas 78230
www.halopublishing.com
contact@halopublishing.com

For Solomon & Adeline,
you are the dreamer of dreams
and the inspiration for imagination...

Solomon was an ordinary boy with an ordinary family.

He liked his parents...

He liked his sister...

He liked his cat...

And...he liked his dog.

Solomon seemed happy...

But...there were things in the world that
Solomon didn't like to do because he feared them.

Solomon thought long and hard about how he could
solve this problem. Then, he had a great idea!
He would invent a special robot that would do
all the things he feared doing around the house.

Solomon went right to work and built an amazing
robot that looked almost exactly like Solomon...
but it was not Solomon. It was...a robot.

Solomon wanted to try his invention out right away. The first thing that came to his mind was vacuuming. He hated vacuuming for his mommy and daddy because he didn't like the loud noise the vacuum made when it was turned on.

So, the robot went right to work and began doing his chore for him. Success! Solomon jumped up and down.

The robot began doing all the things around the house that Solomon was afraid of doing. This was great!

COURAGE

Solomon was proud of his invention.
His robot had something he had
trouble having on his own...
Courage.

Solomon became great friends with his invention. He loved his robot because he was doing all the scary things around the house. But...there was a bigger problem.

Solomon was having trouble making new friends at school because he was too afraid to talk to his classmates.

So, Solomon decided he no longer needed to
go to school. His robot could go for him.

When the robot arrived at school, none of Solomon's classmates could tell it was not Solomon.

13

Solomon's robot quickly became popular at school because the robot was very **brave** and could do everything that Solomon was afraid to do.

When the robot returned home, it told Solomon about how much **fun** it had with the new **friends** it made.

Solomon was glad that the robot was doing so well at school. But then, Solomon became sad. He realized he was missing out on meeting new **friends** and having **fun.**

Then, Solomon had another great idea!
He decided to be brave like the robot
and go to school himself.

So, the next day, Solomon went back to school.
This time he was brave and showed courage.
He talked to his classmates and wasn't afraid anymore.

He realized how easy it was to make friends once he stopped being afraid. He even started talking more to his teachers.

When Solomon returned home, he told his robot about how much **fun** he had at school. The robot was happy for him because now Solomon was **brave** too.

Solomon thanked his robot for showing him how to have **courage** and to never be afraid.

Now Solomon has a bunch of new friends and
is excited about going to school every day.

Solomon and his robot make a great team and look forward to having more adventures together soon!

the
end

CPSIA information can be obtained
at www.ICGtesting.com
Printed in the USA
LVHW071429290320
651552LV00022B/1253